Ragged Bears

First published in Great Britain in 1998
by Ragged Bears Limited,
Ragged Appleshaw, Andover, Hampshire SP11 9HX

A CIP record of this book is available from the British Library

ISBN 1 85714 153 9
Printed in Hong Kong

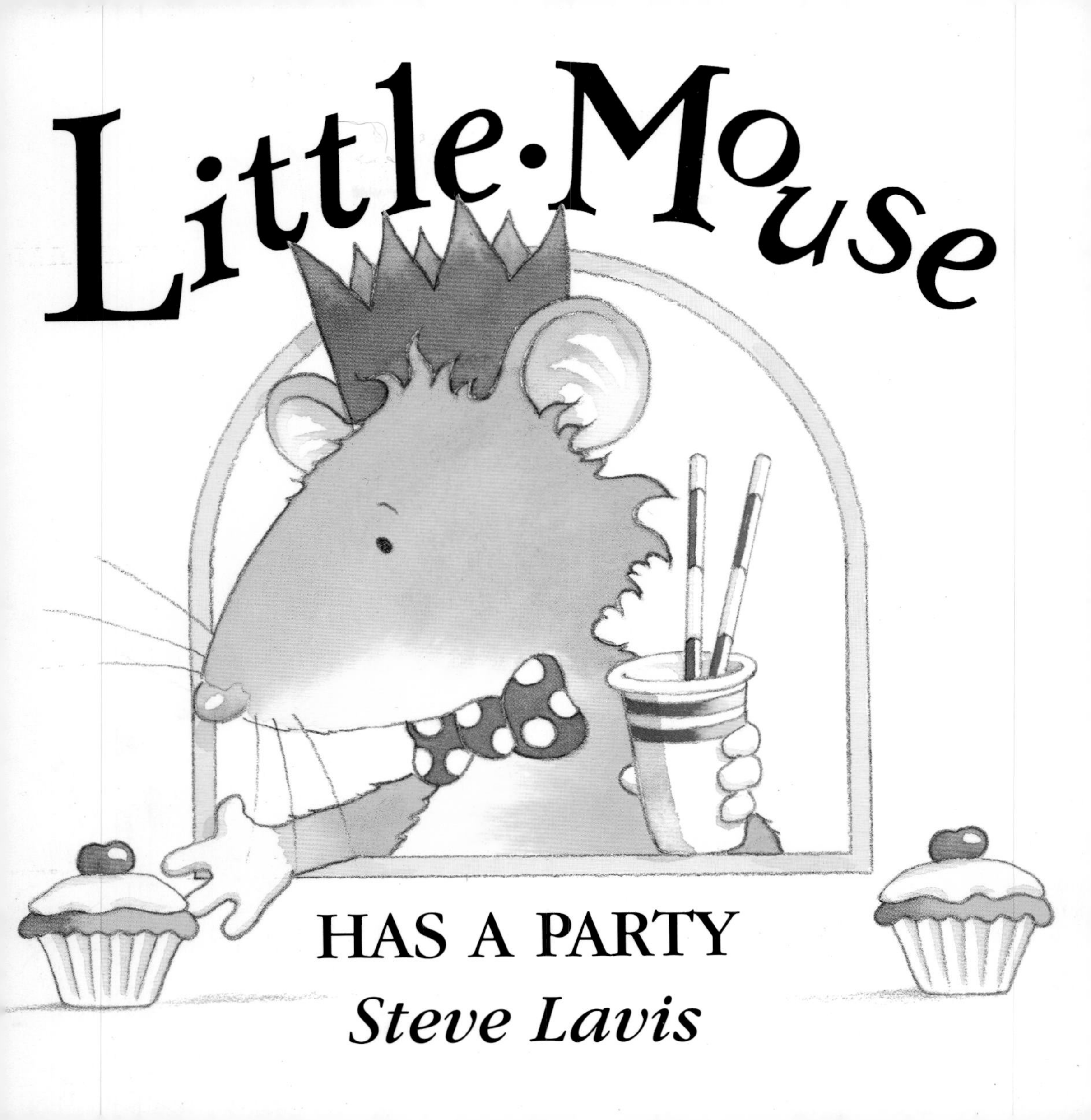
Little Mouse
HAS A PARTY
Steve Lavis

Little Mouse is going to have a party. So, on **Monday** he wakes up early.

On **Tuesday**
he cleans the house.

On **Wednesday**
he goes shopping.

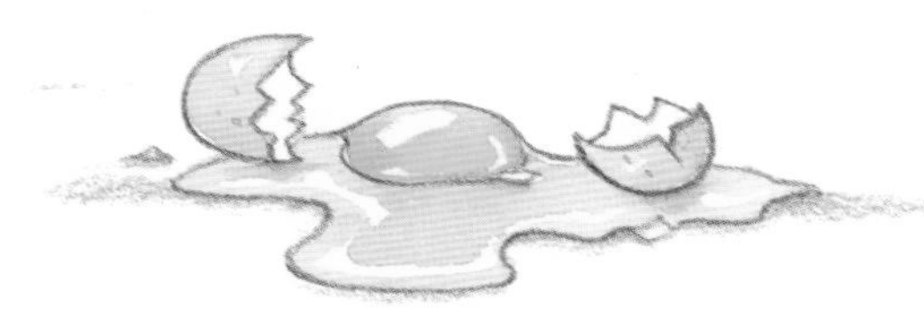

On Thursday
he bakes some cakes.

On **Friday**
he blows up balloons.

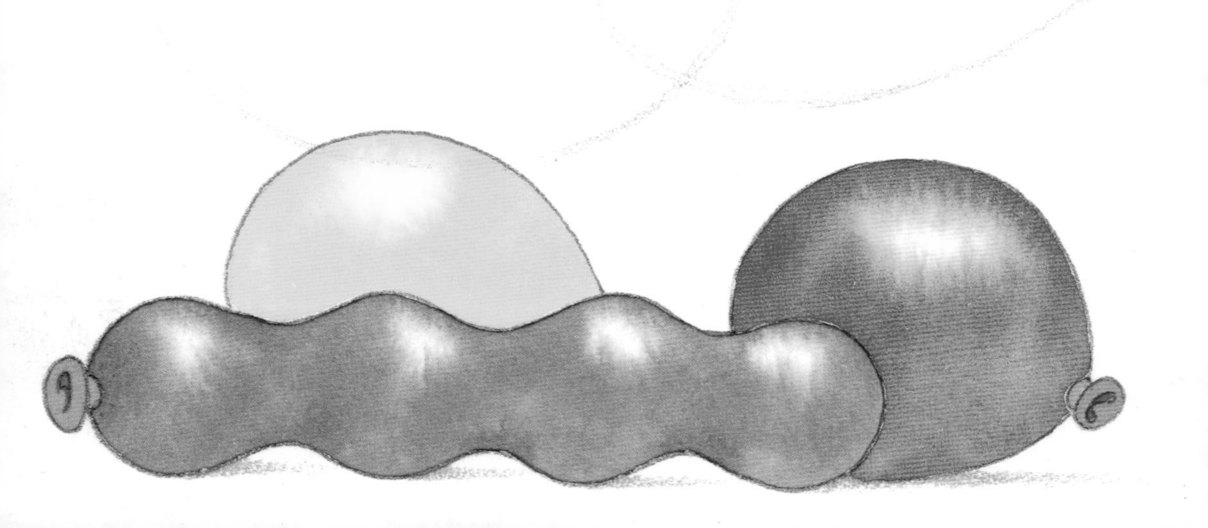

On **Saturday**
he decorates the house.

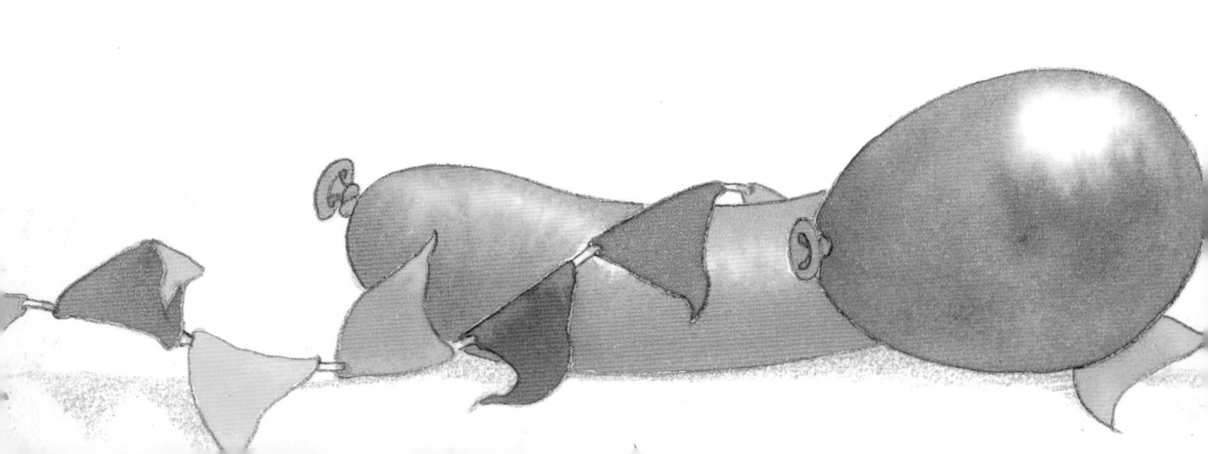

On **Sunday**
he is ready.
Little Mouse is
having a party...

TODAY!